RIME

of the

MODERN

MARINER

an

American

Odyssey

Stephen

Kryska

D1057778

Art by Emily Kryska
Advice by Clark Kryska
Proofing by Jane Kryska

Dedicated to P.C.W. Davies 1995

RIME OF THE MODERN MARINER

AN AMERICAN ODYSSEY

A yachtsman and his crew sail from Buffalo across the Great Lakes destined for Chicago. The cruise degenerates into a philosophical trip of mythical proportions.

CONTENTS

PART 1 – High Moon

Behold the Modern Mariner
invading the den of three
narcotic men who dwell beside
an eerie inland sea.

The Mariner observes each druggie
when, to their surprise,
by chance he chooses one of three
by pointing at him suddenly;
alarmed, Sylvester cries,

"Dear Mariner, why aim at me?
What is it that I've done?"
To this his frightened buddies holler,
"All things under the sun!"

"Come follow me," the Mariner orders,
then he disappears.
Sylvester rises from his cushion
counter to his fears.

Intrigued he leaves and hurries to
the beach beyond a dune.
Above the sandy crest appears,
as if on cue, the moon.

Sylvester labors to the crest,
descends the sandy slope
and finds the Mariner who waits
as solemn as a pope.

"What are you doing? What'd I do?"
Sylvester begs, "Tell me."
The tempted Mariner responds
by pointing to the sea.

"You didn't do enough," he warns,
then dashes down the shore.
Suspecting he may be a boon
Sylvester smiles at the moon,
pursues his visitor.

They lope along the lathered line,
Sylvester never far
behind the Mariner who crashes
through a paddy of reeds and splashes
out across a bar.

"Slow down," Sylvester fulminates,
"I'll have a cardiac."
And still the tireless Mariner flees,
not once does he look back.

A beat before Sylvester drops
the Mariner stops and cries,
"You see it? There!" He aims his arm
to where the sun will rise.

Sylvester staggers to his side
exhausted, "What'd you see?"
"Too much," he answers, "far too much
for anyone but me

because," he now reveals, "I'm
an image mirroring Man.
His brighter half which he defaces,
surreptitiously embraces,
cowers from yet always chases—
Catch me if you can."

"I can't!" And so the Mariner,
through sympathy or guile,
defers by recommending, "Then
perhaps we'll walk a while."

"And talk," Sylvester adds as they
begin to ambulate
beside the sea which whispers to
the apprehensive druggie, 'You
will soon learn of your fate.'

"Regard the moon," the Mariner starts,
"The mask of everyone
is mirrored in that looking glass.
Behind it shines the sun—

Man's brighter half." He follows in
a whisper, "Ah, its light
reflected off that pseudo surface
brightens each one's night."

"I see I see!" Sylvester cheers.
The Mariner replies,
"You certain, boy? You see the moon,
or is there something hot and high
at noon that hits your eyes?"

Before Sylvester can respond,
the fervid Mariner
completely in command continues,
"Hear this: It's for sure

old Adam had ambition, boy,
desire to be free
of all the inhibitions that
suppressed his potency.

But when he exercised his will
and resolutely faced
up to the awesome image whom
he blindly once embraced,

he saw his own enormity.
So aching for relief
from witnessing himself again,
old Adam took a leaf

to mask his masculinity,
but failed to conceal
effectively the presence of
his dominant allele.

Now all his progeny who have
inherited his awe
discover when in reverie
a clue to the identity
of what their sire saw.

Consider when they happen by
a mirror, how solemnly
they contemplate their image then
soliloquize, 'It's me

you're staring at, but who are you,
what is your real name?
It's similar to mine and yet
it's somehow not the same.

Perhaps I'll never know,' they tell
themselves then humbly touch
the chilling surface of the mirror
to smooth away an ancient tear;
too late they see the self-inflicted
smear then whirl away in fear
and wail, 'Life's too much!'

Again at night when they reflect
upon the moon or star,
they visualize themselves a spark
surrounded by the timeless dark.
'Is this,' they ruefully remark,
'the way things really are?'

No!" the Mariner erupts,
"Their moonlight won't expire
unless the sun decides it's time
for ice instead of fire.

But never mind defeatists who
complain that it's too late
to comprehend their relevance,
when all it takes is commonsense
to lead in life's debate,

to see beyond a star, beyond
the moon's passivity.
But like old Adam they're too meek
to penetrate the mirror and peek
behind—Look up at me!"

He grabs Sylvester's turtleneck.
"Do you know what I've seen?
A year ago I sailed west
aboard a yacht and took the test
that Adam had—Why look so sad?
You shouldn't, boy, you should be glad.
I proved I wasn't second best!
Cheer up, here's what I mean":

The Mariner releases him.
Exploding with a laugh
he stabs his finger at the druggie,
"I'm your better half!"

"Oh no." "Oh yes," the Mariner
retorts triumphantly,
then yielding, the Mariner,
with ambiguity

proposes to Sylvester, "We
could argue 'til we're hoarse.
Review instead the firmament.
Perhaps by morning I'll assent
when Nature takes its course."

Immediately he pulls a bottle
from his pocket, "Dawn
is hours away my boy, by then
this gin or you'll be gone."

He swallows slowly several times,
salutes Sylvester, winks.
Sylvester reaches for the bottle,
desperately he drinks.

"You like it, boy?" Sylvester gives
the bottle back, "Oh jeezes,"
he manages to interject
between his puffs and wheezes.

Recovered now, Sylvester queries,
"What's that 'bout a boat?"
"A yacht!" the Mariner replies,
then drinks and clears his throat:

===

★ Stephen Kryska ★

PART 2 – Bon Voyage Not

There was an eager crew of five
all answering to me:
Priscilla, Carmen, Stanislaw
plus Clark and Emily.

They each accepted their assignment
tending to my yacht
whose name was in remembrance of
the Lady of Shalott.

She was a captive of tradition,
fooled by her belief
that her reality must be
reflected in a mirror or she
would never find relief.

Like her I tired of the view
we haplessly embrace,
that we are not equipped to see
the meaning of reality
(a 'petty pace' philosophy
unworthy of our race).

My stage, a full-keeled monohull
twelve meters stem to stern,
was certified a Spirit class,
a watercraft few could surpass,
ensuring our return.

And so with confidence we stored
our gear below the deck
in preparation for our cruise.
I made the final check.

The wind was steady, we were ready
before the break of day.
The sails billowed, snapping taut,
I sang, 'We're on our way!'

With curse and shout we worked her out
due west from Buffalo.
And as the city's towers, rank
by rank, would twinkle out I'd thank
the wind that made it so.

But when the city's halo slipped
beneath the dawning sea,
a flame inside of me expired
simultaneously

then flared anew for in our wake
the morning sun appeared.
My crew of five shalomed the shine,
together we all cheered.

'Break out your bottles, everyone,'
I gestured, 'Here's to life!'
My date, Priscilla, hollered, 'Host,
toast to what I want the most,
to be your legal wife!'

In jest the other couples clinked
their bottles, laughed and drank.
'Your benefactor? Never, Dear.
I'd rather walk the plank!'

So higher, higher every day
until the end of June
we drank, each one of us behaving
like a buzzed buffoon.

===

Sylvester hiccups once, twice;
abashed, grins ear to ear,
then braces for the impact of
what he's about to hear.

===

Chicago was our destination.
To a silly song
our voices trilled, the bottles spilled,
the breeze blew us along.

We all felt good. I knocked on wood
when finally the haze
began to burn away at last.
It had for several days

completely screened the coast which I
had blindly navigated.
So naturally when land appeared
I was surprised, elated

and humbled too because I knew
as skipper of a yacht,
indulging in excessive drinking
would degenerate my thinking.
Swearing I would not

I crossed my heart then pulled the log
and promptly started writing
After sailing blind for days
we've now had our first sighting

of Ohio's coastline on
this fourth day of July
when Carmen interrupted me
while logging in my entry—'Si,
there Cleveland, captain, aye.'

I aimed my glass and saw the city;
something wasn't right.
A cloud of smoke concealed the central
district dark as night.

'La algarada,' Carmen claimed,
'A riot maybe, no?'
I checked my chart and marked the spot,
'I really don't think so.'

The city (off our port side) passed
about two miles south.
My reading from the chart made clear
polluted waters smoldered near
the Cuyahoga's mouth.

I watched until the city slowly
dwindled to a speck,
then steered Shalott northwest and saw
far out beyond the deck

the slow and sly beginning of
a summer storm that grew
until a waterspout appeared.
I blinked and there were two.

Then three, four, five! They all
developed from the first
so deviously that I could sense,
or thought I did, intelligence
controlling them. I cursed

for now the eerie waterspouts
like fingers on a hand
curled over and crushed a distant ship!
I shouted this command:

'Reduce the sails, everyone,
a storm's approaching. Hurry!'
My merry mates were drunk from drinking.
Someone yelled, 'Why worry?'

'The storm! The sails!' I complained,
but they just laughed at me.
The waves began to rise and grow
and hiss! the wind was blowing so.
I boiled like the sea.

The sky went black, the sails clacked
exploding from the strain,
then suddenly the wheel went slack.
I tried but couldn't bring it back
when it began to rain.

It pounded, poured, the wind it roared,
I bellowed, 'Without fail
to the cabin! Take my word
or argue with a gale!'

My word was taken seriously
above the stormy din,
but panicking, my crew forgot
to take their share of gin.

We scrambled down the cabin stairs
and huddled on the floor.
I wondered, with the wheel lost
would we crash on the shore,

or perish in the sea that boiled
like a witch's brew?
I feared our fate was sealed when
that raging storm it grew

and grew within my mind until
I saw myself up high
above the state of Michigan.
My viewpoint in the sky

revealed the peninsula
shaped like an open hand
of some primeval sculptor who
had signatured the land.

The scene began to spin and I
was spiraling to my grave.
I reached and found Priscilla's hand
preparing her, 'Be brave.'

We tumbled, tossed and turned were lost
within the stormy grip
that carried us away on what
would be our final trip.

'I hate to say it, everyone.
It looks like our last call.'
Priscilla motivated screamed,
'There's rubbing alcohol!'

She scrambled forward to the head,
the others followed after,
then all at once I heard their chilling
cries and bouts of laughter—

laughter laced with gallows humor
signaling their fate;
five cripples lost without their crutch,
reality had proved too much,
all I could do was wait

which wasn't long. A cry from the
compartment split the air,
'There's absolutely nothing in
the cabinet, just medicine
and water everywhere!'

Then everyone in panic mode
began to thrash around
the cramped compartment at the head
then silence, not a sound

except my broken heart as I
imagined their demise,
and shuddered at the likelihood
of what would meet my eyes

when I would be confronted by
a sight too cruel to bear,
their beaten bodies dying because
their spirits didn't care.

'I care!' I cried and on my feet
proceeded to the door
and forced it open to what I
had conjured up before,

the tangled bodies of my crew.
The scene could not be worse,
their heads against the toilet bowl,
a toxic tombstone, bless each soul,
and my Shalott a hearse!

I stood in silent sorrow when
an arm of someone shook
and shooed me to a shelf on which
my bible rested. With a twitch
I grabbed the bogus book

and ripped the cover open then
pulled out the bottle inside,
and drank to keep from joining those
who didn't drink and died.

PART 3 – Pelee Point
Counterpoint

The storm was over now. Another
troubled me anew
within my mind, a hawk and dove
conflicted as they flew

in opposition arguing
exactly who's at fault.
Should I have blithely shared my gin
or not? So is it now a sin?
The hawk aired his assault

against the dove who rendered her
opinion that my vice
was my abject refusal to
attempt to help my panicked crew
by my self-sacrifice.

About to lose the argument
I heard her pleading voice
reminding me about the risk
inherent in each choice.

The hawk demurred, to reassess
the verdict he had sought.
The dove retreated to my heart
to keep from getting caught

in case the hawk asserted his
superiority.
I felt the worry of her wings
against my rib, the troubled things
of her uncertainty

like Eve who worried would she be
the winner of a pardon.
Despite her independent thought
her hope for mercy was for naught;
she lost her treasured garden.

Her lesson wasn't lost on me.
I valued it and so...
despite my doubt, however odd,
in the existence of a god,
I took a chance, proceeded to nod
Amen, when I heard 'No!'

I pivoted once, twice—Christ!
There was no one around,
no one alive at least, then who
or what had made that sound?

I flew upstairs, fell on the deck
frozen stiff with fear,
then rolling over on my side—
'What am I seeing? No!' I cried
so loud the dead could hear.

I saw a foreign object heading
directly toward Shalott.
It vanished, reappeared again,
it was and then was not.

I rolled up off the deck and goggled
at its growing cast.
A coastguard cutter came at me
and it was coming fast.

I stood entranced as it advanced,
afraid I'd be accused
of homicide. Was I to blame
when crime and guilt are not the same?
I'd never be excused.

I hurried down the cabin stairs
intentionally to hide.
On second thought I hauled each body
up, then over the side.

Each body sank as bubbles in
procession slowly rose
up to the surface of the sea.
The bubbles broke with this decree:
'Your book of life doeth close.'

'You over there! Need any help?'
I cowered around to find
the cutter off the starboard side.
Around my mouth I cupped my hands
and cried, 'No, never mind!'

It seemed forever waiting for
an answer, then it came.
'Well carry on. Good luck to you
and pass the greeting to your crew.
Good sailing in God's name!'

The cutter sped toward Canada,
it dwindled to a dot.
I blinked my eyes, it disappeared,
I scanned my battered yacht.

The mainsail and the jib were gone,
the mast was stripped and bare,
my custom boom a memory,
the wheel beyond repair.

Shalott without her rigging was
unstable as a scow.
So what, dejectedly I asked
myself, should I do now?

Of course, I answered, held my breath
then hurriedly went aft.
The inboard was no worse for wear.
I set the starter, said a prayer—
The engine roared! I laughed

then improvised a makeshift tiller
from a broken spar,
confirmed by GPS that Pelee
Point was not too far,

then aimed Shalott for sanctuary
forty miles west
and raced full throttle with the engine
passing every test.

The waning sun was in my eyes,
below the bow he fell,
then waved goodbye and slowly sank
as I sank into Hell.

The haloed moon like one huge eyeball
hovered overhead;
she blinked when drifting clouds would break
her stare and still I fled.

Then stars like predators appeared
in packs locked on a scent;
they tracked the engine's smoky trail—
faster, faster I went.

The droning engine mesmerized
me as I raced along,
its sound inducing memories
of our seafaring song,

the song we sang when we were sailing
on the eerie sea.
The song was all too loud and clear,
the singers too alive and near;
I muttered, 'Go, get out of here,
bug off and let me be.'

I blocked my aching ears and pulled
my head down to my knees,
but they remained within my mind,
the haunting memories

that frolicked like a gang of spirits
weird and white as bone:
The memories of bottles popping
memories of parties stopping
memories of bodies dropping
'Please leave me alone!'

'You are alone,' a voice replied.
I tossed my head up screaming;
awakening, I realized
that I was only dreaming.

The moon and stars were still above
and I was speeding west.
Except for them I was alone.
Besides the engine's dreary drone
the other sound was all my own,
the drumming in my chest.

An hour or more flew by before
I recognized the scene
upon the purple moonlit waves:
An iridescent sheen

of weathered wings from butterflies
that traveled in a swarm
until their migratory flight
was canceled by the storm.

Then Pelee can't be far, I thought,
Soon I'll have some gin.
I stood straight up and faced the moon
declaring, 'I'll be there soon
and drink to where I've been.'

She glowered down at me offended
by my brazen cry:
'The cops will never catch me there
in Canada, ha-ha, that's where,
so go on Moon and stare, stare!'
I spat up in her eye

then settled in my seat and steered
Shalott along the waste.
The eerie sea surprisingly
grew sticky just like paste.

The sewage from the industries,
the sulfur, gas and oil
beneath the eyeball's pale heat
began to burn and boil.

The bow was chiseling through the water.
Sparks shot overhead
and riddled the entire deck
with blisters glowing red.

Behind me in the distance I
could hear the hissing wake
that undulated in the moonlight
like a Mayan snake.

A halyard flying from the mast
reported like a whip,
and every single time that halyard
cracked my heart would skip.

'Shut up!' I yelled repeatedly
'til I heard no replies.
I rubbed the stubble on my chin
then yawned and closed my eyes

when suddenly the engine sputtered,
coughed and gasped for air,
then died, it died, died. I didn't
breathe, I didn't dare

move any muscle, blink or think.
The night closed in around.
I was a fugitive. Cliché
or not, I had been found.

Instinctively responding to
my sudden urge to hide,
I hurried to the cabin door
and flung it open wide.

I slipped and sailed down the steps
crash landing on the floor.
I lay there for one painful moment
then, I knew no more.

PART 4 – Trick or Treat

When I recovered consciousness
and staggered to my feet,
I wondered if I had been dead
the pain was so complete.

Embracing the philosophy
of breathing à la Zen,
I exercised the moves until
my strength returned again.

Recovered now, I scaled the stairs
and squinting in the light,
I stood aghast for everything
I saw was dazzling white.

The deck, the cabin roof, the sea
were blanketed with snow!
My burning eyes were shedding tears
when they began to grow

accustomed to the brilliancy
that perfectly disguised
a dock? a shack? a chimney stack?
I swanned my arms and bended back—
Detroit materialized!

I rubbed my eyes in disbelief
afraid of going blind,
or was I just hallucinating,
did I lose my mind?
            ===
"Oh no," Sylvester disagrees,
"You have the finest mind
that I have ever come across
or ever hope to find,

and Mariner, remember that
you pointed straight at me;
between us three your eyes I drew,
I'm sure that you can see."
            ===
Stiff and stupefied I stood,
stared at the waterfront,
then for a better look refocused,
keen to start the hunt.

I scanned the Motor City scene
uncertain it was real.
What happened to the eerie sea,
what did the snow conceal?

Shalott was parked on river ice
some twenty yards from shore.
I guessed it would support my weight.
Deciding to explore

I dangled from a rail and dropped.
The ice it didn't crack.
I eased across the twenty yards
afraid of looking back.

I landed on a riverwalk
adjacent to a park
where plaza lights snapped on in time
with the approaching dark.

On higher ground a building loomed.
Inscribed on its façade
were poignant words *Old Mariners' Church*
where I saw something odd:

Five seagulls at a Gothic window
perched along its sill,
and in their pale midst a crow
whose look gave me a chill,

reminding me about the legend
where it has been said,
to right a wrong The Crow will bring
a soul back from the dead.

I pondered its significance,
then noticed down the street
a portal to the tunnel where
Detroit and Windsor meet.

With Canada directly south
my world was upside down.
I've had enough, I told myself,
It's time to leave this town.

I headed east in search of peace,
dismay is what I found:
Abandoned buildings, shuttered shops,
parading girls at taxi stops
indifferent to indifferent cops,
corruption all around.

Then sirens in the neighborhoods
beyond the downtown blight
began to sound, informing me
that houses burned for all to see—
Could it be Devil's Night?

Eventually I saw ahead,
high on a warehouse wall,
a billboard of a burlesque queen
in costume meant for Halloween
exposed behind her shawl.

I paused, for a moment thought
about my merry mates.
A neon sign distracted me,
it blinked *Hotel Cheap Rates*.

So like the moth attracted to
a flame I hurried for
that bleak hotel, and reaching it
I found beside the door

a news rack filled with Sunday papers;
some were quite bizarre.
I came across a late edition
of the *Windsor Star*.

My jaw dropped, my heart stopped,
I held my buzzing head.
The paper had my picture and
beneath *This Man Found Dead*.

===

"Oh no no no," Sylvester whines,
"Why do you say such things?"
He wraps his scrawny arms around
the Mariner and clings.

The Mariner ignores the druggie.
Anchored in a state
of painful reminiscence he
continues to relate:

                    ===

I fell against the door defeated,
'God, it can't be me!'
then slammed my fist just as the door
flew open suddenly.

I blundered in and caught my balance
on a banister.
A wafting voice welcomed me,
'Hello Mariner.'

I spun around to face the voice.
Within the shadows hid
the perfumed presence of a women.
Silently she slid

in to the light that seeped beneath
a lone hotel room door.
Her silhouette encouraged me,
I wanted to see more.

'Come follow me,' she whispered then
sashayed on down the hall.
She slipped in to the room and so
I moved along the wall,

but when I reached the point where she
went in the room I found
no trace of her, no room or door,
just walls, walls all around!

I rushed out to the lobby shaking
like a nervous wreck.
Before I had a chance to exit,
something grabbed my neck

and dragged me down that hallway to
my rendezvous with Hell.
I grappled with the gagging grip,
my tongue began to swell.

I fought to save my screaming lungs;
my efforts were in vain
when thankfully unconsciousness
relieved me of my pain.

PART 5 – Hang Over

When someone dreams it often seems
that one is wide awake.
I dreamt that I was in the Arctic
frozen to a stake.

And in that dream a sun appeared,
the ice began to melt,
my deadened nerves returned to life,
the warming rays I felt.

I opened up my thawing eyes
then shut them just as quick.
It's not a dream, I told myself,
The dream was just a trick!

===

"What did you see? Tell me, tell me."
The Mariner replies,
a combination of repose
and jitter in his eyes:

===

I was tied against the mast
with rope so tight it hurt;
the pressure was so forceful it
was pressing through my shirt;

against my chest I felt a weight;
I looked below my chin
and saw a bottle hung on me,
the brand was *Death's Door* gin.

Depressed, I said goodbye to life,
Farewell, Adieu, Amen,
convinced my time to leave the world
was then then then.

===

"Oh please I pray don't talk that way.
What if it all comes true?"
The Mariner contains himself,
"Allow me to get through."

===

Shalott shook, shuddered and with
a screech slid on the ice.
A chorus of angry voices shouted,
'He shall pay the price!'

I looked up focusing ahead:
Five figures on the deck
implied the price to pay must be
in blood, not cash or check.

Over the river ice we crashed,
me and that hostile five
who shifted to improve their view—
My God! It was my crew, my crew
 but they were not alive!

Priscilla, Carmen, Stanislaw
plus Clark and Emily
together, all of us again!
So what became of me?

Could it be possible, at the
hotel where I was mugged,
that witchy woman somehow tricked
me into getting drugged,

preventing me from recognizing
fantasy from fact?
I still could see and feel and hear,
my senses seemed intact.

Whatever actually occurred,
alive or dead, my crew
was resurrected without doubt,
the fantasy was true.

They gathered in a semi-circle
gladly holding hands,
and as Priscilla ordered them,
they skipped to her commands.

Then suddenly Priscilla stopped.
She was a sight to see.
She pointed to the south and swelled
her buxom breast then with a burst
she yelled, 'Remember me?'

An awful grin curled on her mouth
as she returned to dance.
I banged my head against the mast.
I didn't have a chance.

I watched them whirl and twirl until
my eyes danced in my head.
They stopped, scrambled to the bow.
I wondered what would happen now
when I saw far ahead:

Detroit's white river widening;
beyond, a greenish glare.
I blinked my eyes, to my surprise
we were in Lake Saint Claire.

Shalott maintained a steady course
across the growling ice,
as if her glide was powered by
some magical device.

I swung my head, looked to the left,
green ice floes sailed past.
I swung my head, looked to the right,
green ice was flowing fast.

And from the corner of my eye
I saw Priscilla turn.
She seared me with her fiery stare
until I thought I'd burn.

She clutched her throat and caterwauled,
'No alcohol was in
the cabinet, just medicine
and baby aspirin!'

She turned and laughed derisively
joined by her faithful four
who all together faced me shouting,
'We dropped to the floor!'

'You panicked! I lost all control.
I'm not the one to blame!'
The four tossed back their heads and jeered;
to me Priscilla came.

I squirmed and struggled at the mast,
'Priscilla, set me free.'
Unmoved, she carped, 'You S.O.B.,
you dumped me in the sea.'

'What choices did I have?' I asked,
'You didn't take your gin.'
Her green eyes flashed with anger then
they gradually grew thin.

'No matter what you think,' she bragged,
'I'm not the least naïve.'
She slapped the bottle—'My, how sad,
the bogus bible's where you had
this drink I do believe.'

'And I believe,' I countered, 'you
were warned about the storm.
You should have taken your supply.
The deadly weather last July
you knew was not the norm.'

Provoked, Priscilla faced the north,
'Size up this storm instead.'
Intimidating me she shouted,
'Huron! Raise your head!'

Far in the north horizon far
above the lake I saw
a wondrous waterspout appear—
Her faithful four began to cheer.
That spout became a jaw!

And then a gaping mouth took form,
two nostrils flaring red.
A nose, and then two eyes evolved,
two blazing evil eyes revolved
on the face of a hideous head!

It yawned, inhaling, drawing up
Shalott with us on board.
I stretched to see and recognized
below us as we soared:

The Straits of Mackinac, Saint Marys
River and Soo Locks,
with southbound freighters wintering
at iced-in shipping docks.

The next thing I remember we
were falling from the sky.
Shalott slammed on an ice pack.
I was certain that I'd die.

But no, soon as I caught my breath,
Shalott slid on the ice
and plunged in water black as coal.
A frenzied holler ripped my soul,
'He shall pay the price!'

That mad decree alerted the sea.
It began to boil and roar.
Clouds rolled across the sky and thunder
clapped 'til my ears were sore.

Then like a horse on its hind legs
Shalott stood on her keel.
She dropped and shot like an arrow hot
from a bow made of cold steel.

My head slammed back against the mast
caused by the sudden start.
I screamed and hollered 'til I thought
my lungs would blow apart.

'What happened? Tell me! Where are we?
How much must I endure?'
Priscilla humored me, 'Relax,
it's Lake Superior.'

★ Stephen Kryska ★

PART 6 – Apostle Impossible

As I hung fast against the mast
like meat strung on a spit,
Shalott forged on without a hint
that she would ever quit.

She splashed along a narrow lead
with ice on either side,
sliced through the waters of a calm
polynya acres wide,

then over fields of slush and sludge,
across a fractured floe
where several ice volcanoes near
the shore began to blow.

High as a house they hissed and fizzed.
Because of their location
the pressure waves beneath the ice
induced their loud aeration.

Another noise just off our starboard
side began to sound,
caused by the keeled back for which
the sturgeon is renowned.

The fish was scraping with its back
the clear ice as it swam,
producing an incessant *clack*
just like a snapping clam.

An ancient bottom dweller fostered
by a primal power,
the fish came up to visit me
as if to offer company
in my ill-fated hour.

It was a gesture, Nature's way
of saying, I assumed,
endurance and performance will
reward by helping us fulfill
our end, or else we're doomed.

I will endure! I will perform!
My thoughts were loud and clear.
Priscilla sensed my zeal remarking,
'Something's fishy here.'

She held her nose, 'I smell a hint
of misplaced sympathy.'
Then reaching for her hair—I froze—
she stretched a red strand by her nose
and standing in a mocking pose
declared, 'I pity thee.'

I bowed my head and watched her feet
then asked, 'Where are we going?'
She slapped the bottle, answering,
'To islands always glowing.'

Her toes curled when she answered me.
I asked, 'And where are they?'
She slapped the bottle, curled her toes,
'Oh, they're not far away.'

She slapped again, her feet were gone,
I watched my medal swing;
then I reacted with a laugh,
it seemed the damndest thing,

that cursed bottle on my chest
suspended by the rope,
reminding me about the costly
price we pay for hope.

I closed my eyes to calm myself
debating should I pray,
while the bottle ticked and tocked
my luckless life away.

Just like a clock in time it stopped,
a dead weight on my neck.
I opened up my eyes and saw
upon it was a speck.

It sparkled like a flake chipped off
a thousand suns in June
that melted in a ball and then
solidified at noon.

The sparkling speck reflected off
the bottle dazzled me.
I jerked my head up wondering
what marvel would I see.

I wasn't disappointed I
was overwhelmed with awe.
The sun was gloried with a crown
defying natural law.

A nest of spikes protruded from
his ornamented head.
They burned as brightly as his face
and straight for them we sped.

The crew in sheer anticipation
danced excitedly.
Priscilla spun away and in
a second was on me.

Controlling her elation she
announced, 'We're almost there.'
I didn't speak or even blink,
replied with just a stare.

'You poor ole thing,' she sympathized,
'No interest in your fate?'
I gulped then asked, 'Enlighten me.'
She blurted out triumphantly,
'Apostle Islands, mate!'

She slapped the bottle, turned and joined
the four in one great bound.
They watched the glorious sun descend,
too moved to make a sound.

The sun went down and yet the spikes
remained bright as before,
so bright despite the distance my
unshaded eyes were sore.

I watched in wonder as the spikes
with each advancing mile
grew larger as we plunged ahead.
Priscilla turned to me and said
with her inviting smile,

'Apostle Islands, take a look!'
They took me by surprise.
Those spikes were definitely islands
there before my eyes.

PART 7 – Scheming Dreams

The glowing archipelago
was flooded in a light
that my eyes slow and steadily
adjusted to 'til I could see
with nearly perfect sight.

Ahead an island soon appeared.
I leaned to have a look.
It could have been a picture taken
from a children's book.

It was encircled by a ring
of water powder blue
that for at least a quarter mile
radiated to

concentric rings of ice in every
color, barring black,
that glistened as if coated in
a glaze of clear shellac.

We drew up closer to the island
at a constant speed,
then slowed as we maneuvered by
when I began to read:

Along the shoreline rising to
the height of fifty feet
were rainbow-colored walls of sandstone
radiating heat

so hot it melted all the snow
that blanketed the deck,
and promptly dried the ragged rope
that scratched my itchy neck.

The island passed behind the stern,
we left its ring of blue
and traveled over rainbow ice
perhaps a mile or two,

when off our starboard side a second
island soon appeared
with pitted walls unlike the first.
Shalott dropped in its ring—I cursed
for there was something weird.

A pair of piercing yellow eyes
within each pit was blinking.
At once my crew began to yell,
exactly why I couldn't tell,
what could they have been thinking?

Their yelling echoed off the walls
so loud I thought they'd crack,
when in a blink the yellow eyes
were gone! the pits went black

as owls erupted from the walls
in one fantastic flock.
The pressure wave from all those flapping
wings gave me a shock.

High overhead the flock flew by,
not making any sound.
Recovering, I took a breath,
began to look around

and saw another island that
exhibited a sheen.
Although we were a mile away
it seemed to be a green,

a vivid color one might find
within an Irish dell.
We minimized the distance close
enough for me to tell

that this Apostle island was
completely overgrown
with moss and scabby lichen that
produced the verdant tone.

We floated by when on a peak
I saw a rock formation,
a sphinx that stared out into space
in secret contemplation.

Shalott maneuvered, realigning
with its steady stare,
then after several anxious moments
sailed through the air

and splashed down in a ring of water
this time deeper blue.
My eyes adjusted from the jolt.
I witnessed something new:

An island where two trunkless legs
of stone like silos stood
next to a head half in the sand
enticing me to understand
its meaning if I could.

On its eroded pedestal
the letters OZ remained
in reference to mythic time
when king and wizard reigned.

The head began to move its hardened
lips and question me:
Would I awaken from my stormy
dream like Dorothy?

Or like king Ozymandias,
the head preferred to know:
Would I despair, defeated by
mistakes made long ago?

Yes! I'm dreaming, No! I'm scheming.
Answering the head,
my daring thoughts were loud and clear
as if they had been said.

Priscilla must have heard somehow.
She came to me and spoke
with passion as she yanked the rope,
'You think it's all a joke?

You'll wake up and we'll all be gone?
Well, let me tell you, mate.
The four behind me at the bow
and I can hardly wait

until the time arrives when we
will even up the score.
Relax ole boy, the time will come
when you will joke no more.'

She spun away and joined the four
who greeted her with glee.
Then looking back at me she shouted,
'To your destiny!'

Shalott responded straight away.
Across the ice she flashed,
then moments later in another
ring of water splashed

and stopped, resumed her course proceeding
peacefully ahead
where on the water was a seething
murk electric red.

We penetrated, entering
a wondrous world inside,
a place where faithful surely would
expect gods to reside.

An island looming in the distance
that we angled for
gave rise to something marvelous
that rose above the shore.

Its awe-inspiring colorscape
defied imagination,
displaying combinations worthy
of a god's creation.

Approaching closer to the shore,
Priscilla shouted, 'Mate,'
then landing, she announced, 'Ta-da!
We're at the Temple Gate!'

PART 8 – Gate Fate

Two pillars with diameters
exceeding seven feet
were posted on the sandy shore
the shade of harvest wheat.

They stood much higher than the mast,
were thirty feet apart,
and in between a scarlet mist
throbbed like a beating heart.

An arch with curious inscriptions
spanned the mist between
the pillars which were shedding, like
the arch, a golden sheen.

The animated energy
emitted by the gate
completely overpowered me.
Priscilla waxed rhapsodically,
'There's more to see, just wait!'

She vaulted from the deck and landed
on the sandy shore,
approached the throbbing gate and waited
for her faithful four

who all together jumped without
a moment's hesitation,
and joined her where they bowed devoutly
seeking inspiration.

Priscilla raised her arms as thunder
broke the sacred silence.
The scarlet mist between the pillars
boiled with a violence

then it was gone, it disappeared,
the view was very clear.
I saw what zealous faithful would
undoubtedly hold dear:

A paradise beyond the gate
reflecting Hebrew lore,
a supernatural locale
where time has no before.

A valley lush with blooms and berries
every bush was bearing,
and every tree and glade was fashioned
with the greatest daring,

and in the center of the valley,
there a gleaming lake
was guarded on its sacred shore
by twenty statues, maybe more
no human hand could make.

The scenery was heavenly,
imbuing me with awe.
My crew along the shore were walking
pointing at the statues, gawking.
Here is what they saw:

A special statue came alive,
a Stranger trim and tall.
My crew encircling him began
to dance around this mighty man
who stood enjoying it all.

He greeted each admirer
and gave a secret sign.
His attitude and body language
bordered on divine.

Events were overwhelming me.
What if I yelled and screamed?
Perhaps the noise would wake me from
this fantasy I dreamed.

Alive or dead? Awake or dreaming?
Questioning what's true
began to waste and worry me.
My life's cruel ambiguity
unnerved me through and through.

I saw myself a sham for Christ
connected to the mast,
my cross that I must bear, but how
much longer would I last?

My crew joined by the Stranger sallied
from the paradise.
He stood before the gate then raised
his arms and waved them twice.

Immediately the mist returned,
then snow fell steadily,
fell on the deck, fell on the shore,
but never fell on me.

Shalott slid from the slippery shore
and quickly backed away.
In preparation for a surge
I braced myself then had the urge
to bow my head and pray.

A cautionary voice like rolling
thunder rumbled 'No!'
I looked around with apprehension
peering through the snow.

My captive crew was at the bow,
the Stranger with them too.
Shalott maneuvered, set a course,
across the ice we flew

as islands that we passed before
were passing in a flash
until the outermost appeared
when I feared we might crash;

but thankfully Shalott recovered,
pulled out of a spin,
careered toward open water then
she gracefully dropped in

and stopped, completely motionless
as any ship would be
if it were mired in the moon's
Sea of Tranquility.

She didn't lean, she didn't list,
she didn't tilt or roll,
just idled at the outer limit
of the islands' glow.

No stars were in the pointless sky,
the moon I failed to see.
My mood compelled me to surrender—
'Someone, pity me!'

As if my cry had power to
determine what I chose,
the east horizon glowed and then
the morning sun arose,

and in the welcomed light I saw
the Stranger on the deck.
His eyes were focused on the bottle
hanging from my neck.

Draped on his shoulder was a net
for fishing I supposed.
This mighty man in person looked
quite peaceful and composed.

He started, stepping toward me
deliberately and slow.
His sandaled feet I noticed left
no footprints in the snow,

full proof he was a member of
the spiritual elite.
What will I say, and what will he
when face to face we meet?

★ Stephen Kryska ★

PART 9 – Guilt Trip

A first step starts a journey of
a thousand miles they say.
I started mine a life ago
when I set sail from Buffalo
and sadly lost my way.

'You need direction, Mariner,'
the Stranger posed as he
took one last step and stood unyielding,
staring straight at me.

'Mind reading is your game?' I asked.
The Stranger, feigning, smiled.
His condescension signified
he saw in me a child

undisciplined, a traveler
adrift with many flaws.
Instead I saw myself a skeptic
quizzing every cause,

relying less on faith to solve
the mystery of things,
and more on reasoning with all
the benefits it brings.

Consider Adam and his faithful
Eve who both were blessed
with benefits they understood
would comfort them the best

provided they obeyed the rules
no matter how unfair.
Renouncing them? They didn't dare
or hardly even care

until at last they recognized
the patent contradiction
of their beliefs, but in the end
rebuffed their own conviction.

Too late for them but not for me.
My spirit wasn't broken.
I stunned the Stranger—Hear my thoughts.
This mariner has spoken!

Confusion and embarrassment
were featured on his face,
an obvious reaction as if
he were sprayed with Mace.

A moment later he recovered.
Positively pious,
he advocated, 'Mariner,
you must reject your bias.'

Continuing, he said, 'I hope
to make you understand.'
He sidled up and kindly touched
my shoulder with his hand

and softly spoke so no one else
but I could hear him speak.
'There is a limit to the times
He turns His other cheek.'

The implication bothered me.
I wished he would explain.
He tried, 'The Master sacrificed
and suffered for your pain.'

'I'm tired of your double-talk.
What else have you to say?'
He answered gravely, 'Follow Him.
There is no other way.'

'You're playing games again,' I charged.
He leaned down in my face
and growled, 'A stubborn mariner
like you is a disgrace.'

With bulging eyes and blushing face
his anger was complete.
He jerked the net clear off his shoulder,
threw it at my feet,

produced my bible from his tunic,
opened up its cover,
and in the hollow slammed his fist
then warned, 'Love one another!'

His attitude confounded me.
Now what was I to think?
He grabbed the cursed bottle, brought
it to my lips and said, 'You ought
to take this gift and drink.'

'Accept a gift from you?' I scoffed,
'You're not someone I trust.'
He acquiesced, unruffled said,
'We all do what we must.'

He grandiosely walked away
with parting words for me:
'You closed your mind, you locked your heart
and threw away the key.'

I bowed my head and contemplated
what his words could mean,
when on the bottle playing like
a movie was this scene:

A gang of men came into focus
shouting as they ran
along a dusty street; within
their midst I saw a man

bedraggled, plodding painfully.
The mob threw rocks at him.
He bore a cross upon his back.
The scene began to dim.

It faded, flickered, reappeared
with shocking clarity.
The face of every member of
the mob resembled me!

Confused, insulted, horrified,
ashamed to be with men
like those content to brutalize,
I bit my tongue and closed my eyes
then counted up to ten.

I opened them again and saw
a bloodied face this time,
a tortured visage of the Christ,
the victim of the crime.

Another crime of sorts I ventured
might be active here:
Deception perpetrated by
the Stranger with intent to try
and drill in me the fear

that I was guilty, judged and sentenced,
hoping I'd retract
my disbelief and seek redemption,
God, to be exact.

No doubt the Stranger heard my thoughts.
The visage disappeared,
dispelling any guilt I felt,
my conscience had been cleared.

Alarmed, Priscilla like a runner
at a starting bell
sprung to the Stranger begging him,
'Oh please, please let me tell.'

He nodded, so she came to me
and claimed, 'You ain't alive.'
She brought her fist up to my face
and spread it, blurting, 'Five!'

Then pointing at my nose, she crowed,
'And you are number six.'
'Correction, Dear, I'm number one,
accustomed to your tricks.'

Priscilla smirked, 'You think so, huh?
Hello! You're very dead.
Remember in Detroit, the river,
did you feel the cold and shiver?
Think of what I said.

And even now, the snow and ice,
it's cold in the extreme.'
I told her, 'Darling, stay with me,
you're just a vivid dream.'

'A nightmare, Dear,' she said then slapped
the bottle as she smiled.
She huffed and puffed to show her stuff
behaving like a child.

Approving of her act, a cheer
erupted from the four.
The Stranger clapped his hands and warned,
'Enough! I'll have no more.'

(Priscilla always was dramatic.
More than just a friend,
her foibles notwithstanding I
will miss her in the end.)

The Stranger faced the east and raised
his arms above his head.
The sea began to boil and roar
and then the water spread!

A valley was created it
was half a mile wide,
with walls of seething water piled
high on either side.

Then both walls dropped, we were on top
a crest where each wall met,
a crest that rose a mile high.
Priscilla yelled, 'Get set!'

Shalott swooped down and catapulted
us across the sea.
A question still remained unanswered:
What's in store for me?

★ Stephen Kryska ★

PART 10 –Fright Christmas

The risen sun was in my eyes.
He curved across the sky
then dipped and dropped behind me
from his habitat on high.

With equal energy the ice
volcanoes as before
were hissing, fizzing, whizzing by
'til they were heard no more.

Ahead, the lighthouse noted for
its steel frame appeared,
a landmark at the entrance of
the bay some sailors feared.

Well known as Whitefish where a famous
freighter's futile fight
to conquer Lake Superior
proved desperately inferior,
and so it sank one night.

The 'Fitz' to those who worked her was
remembered in a song,
a ballad where her cargo hauling
days went deadly wrong.

Shalott reduced her speed and safely
entered Whitefish Bay,
avoiding pressure ridges as
she squarely made her way

along a channel in the ice
that ended at the Soo
where locks enabled boats to pass.
She chose the port side queue

in line with the Canadian lock
reserved for smaller craft;
American locks were used by vessels
with a deeper draft.

The gates swung open to the chamber
of the foreign lock.
The operator at his station
gave me quite a shock.

He wore a Christmas costume like
Saint Nicholas would wear,
a miter on his head and vestments
bishop red, I swear.

The Stranger noticed my surprise.
'Safe passage through life's locks,'
he cautioned me, 'demands that you
revere the orthodox.'

'Saint Nicholas to you,' I said,
'To me he's Santa Claus.'
The Stranger scoffed, 'A secular
convention fraught with flaws.

Remember, on this holy day
December twenty five,
the time within your heart when Jesus
Christ should come alive,

did you confess that reindeer, jingle
bells and ho ho ho
deserve your adoration? I
heard Yes instead of No.'

The operator honked a horn
to signal our descent.
The water level in the chamber
dropped and so we went

down seven meters slowly to
the waiting world below.
The massive lower gates swung open.
Going with the flow

Saint Marys River hurried us
ice free directly south.
In time we passed by DeTour Village
at the river mouth

and braved the Straits of Mackinac
whose current struck full force.
Shalott engaged the turbulence,
recovered, fixed her course

and headed west straight at the sun
who peered through prison grates,
the ribs and cables of the bridge
that spanned the rampant straits.

I saw myself a prisoner
beginning to believe
my sentence (life-in-death) was true
for which there's no reprieve.

The sun went down behind the bridge.
Each tower like a tree
was decked with merry Christmas lights.
No candy canes or such delights
on this the happiest of nights
were waiting there for me.

We passed beneath the festive bridge
as car lights streamed across.
I filled my lungs and shouted, 'Someone
help me for I'm lost!'

But no one stopped, they were too far
above, too high to hear.
They traveled in a different world
and yet they were so near.

Another time and place, I mused,
then closed my eyes as we
plunged onward to Lake Michigan,
our final inland sea.

Imagining myself a captive
on a pirate ship,
Priscilla was the one to thank
for causing me to walk the plank
and terminate my trip.

I pictured her in pantaloons,
a ruffled blouse and boots;
tucked in her belt a cutlass plus
a pistol packed with animus
ensuring that it shoots.

'Wake up, wake up my buttercup,'
in her facetious way
I heard Priscilla calling, 'Time
to start another day.'

She obviously caught me dreaming.
Pointing to the west
she noted, 'Beaver Island, Dear.
This isn't time to rest.'

On cue the Stranger fervently
began to tell a story
about defenders of their faith
delighting in its glory.

I reinterpreted his view
without nuance or spin.
Familiar with state history,
herewith I now begin:

It was the 1850s when
a man, James Jesse Strang,
the king of Beaver Island and
his flock were ordered to disband
their Mormon homesteads at the hand
of killers and a gang.

The king was ambushed on the harbor
dock, shot in the back,
while Navy witnesses declined
to warn of the attack,

colluding with the killers, some
were given to suspect,
because the killers were resentful
of the Christian sect.

Determined to protect their proper
Christianity,
the mainland faithful raised a gang
and forced the flock to flee.

The Navy witnesses aboard
the warship *Michigan*
allowed the killers sanctuary—
Was it in the plan?

The captain took the killers to
another place where they
were fined, released and feted,
free to live another day.

Today the island village named
in honor of Saint James,
the Mormon maverick crowned as king,
who hoped by God his dream would bring
upon the Earth an Eden Spring,
instead went up in flames.

Religion manufactured in
a Middle Eastern land,
instead of one American made
would never be an equal trade.
I'd buy the homemade brand.

And governing authorities
suspected of collusion,
like many parties ruled by men
leaves me with no illusion.

The Greek named Draco wrote the law
that duly codified
'intention' of a crime as it
applied to homicide.

Assassination of the king
with murderous intent
was clearly how the killers chose
to end the argument.

The federal authorities
involved, allegedly,
could not be trusted in those days
or now considering the ways
they act excessively.

Remember, practice of the law
per the draconian Draco
was typified notoriously
at Ruby Ridge and Waco.

The state and church establishment
when Jesus walked the Earth
opposed his nonconforming views,
their meaning and their worth.

Like him I too have views for which
I grant that I'm not sorry
for giving them, or giving this
my version of the story.

PART 11 – Caring is Believing

The Stranger, having heard my thoughts,
was vexed for being bested
by my revising of his version
that I had contested.

The thesis he espoused, that any
other Christian view
conflicting with the mainstream could
not possibly be true.

And all the discipline imposed
by the establishment
at Saint James, or at other times,
what I would designate as crimes
occurred with its consent.

The Stranger's failed effort to
convince the likes of me
compelled him to administer
reverse psychology:

With warmth he held Priscilla's hand.
To her I heard him say,
'The Mariner may call on God,
the Mariner may pray,

the Mariner may ask for help
but God will never hear.
The Mariner may beg forgiveness,
God will turn His ear.'

Exhausted by my grueling trip,
from all the wear and tear,
too weak to take to task his word
I simply closed my eyes then heard
a distant call *I care!*

I opened them and saw to my
surprise against the sky
a silhouette, a rousing bird
I care! I care! its cry.

It circled round the masthead then
alighted on the peak
and proudly preened its crow black feathers
with a sturdy beak.

And every time Shalott would pitch
that bird percussed the air,
consoling with its ready cry
I care! I care! I care!

I made an effort to reply,
but I was far too weak
to thank the bird, and yet my heart
had strength enough to speak.

This seemed to agitate the Stranger.
Summoning the crew
he pointed at the bird and said,
'It's here to resurrect the dead.
We must give it its due.'

'We what?' Priscilla yelped, to which
the Stranger urged, 'Relent.'
They gathered in a circle and
beside each other hand in hand
around the deck they went.

Eventually the huddle broke.
Priscilla spoke, 'Well I
believe the jerk should suffer more
before we say goodbye.'

In unison the four agreed.
The Stranger, less enthused,
concurred, 'Let Nature take its course.
Consider me recused.'

'It's settled then,' Priscilla ruled.
'Indeed,' the Stranger sighed.
With eyes cast down he shrugged explaining,
'Lord, I truly tried.'

Then looking up, he eyed my friend
the bird perched high above.
The Stranger moved his eyes to mine
and smirked, 'So much for love.'

'Say what you really mean,' I pressed,
'Is that too much to ask?'
He leaned in closer speaking slow,
'To save you was my task,

to sweep you in my net but you
were slippery like an eel.
So now you're in its godless grip,
that bird who will define your trip;
once done, there's no appeal.'

It could be worse, I quipped—a *hiss*
was all the Stranger heard.
My tongue was tied, I tried but couldn't
say a single word.

No matter since I knew the Stranger
read my mind quite well—
my flashback of the sturgeon meeting
me and now the bird's warm greeting.
Clearly I could tell

despite their origins the fish
and bird were unified,
a combination meant to show
that sympathetic Nature low
and high was on my side.

Dismissing my conceit the Stranger
gestured flippantly,
'A quaint conclusion, Mariner.
Enjoy your company.'

By then the day was done when far
ahead a cloud appeared,
or something like it that became
apparent as we neared:

A shoreline power plant with cooling
towers venting veils
of water vapor rising in
the wind like feathered sails.

As excess heated water from
the plant was being purged,
Shalott merged with its westward outflow,
stabilized then surged

straight for the streaked horizon 'til
the moon and stars came out,
when something stunning surfaced in
the middle of our route:

A storm of sparkles shooting up
like mini fireworks,
more evidence of Nature's many
fascinating quirks.

A shoal of silver carp were jumping
to avoid our passing;
their flipping tails, fins and scales
in the moonlight flashing.

I fancied it a ticker tape
parade, a celebration
of chance and evolution, Nature's
version of Creation.

My worldview clearly irked the Stranger;
it was obvious.
Yet he controlled his temperament
and didn't make a fuss.

He simply brought the bottle to
my lips and calmly said,
'Drink this to loosen up your tongue.
Your challenge lies ahead

to tell each person that you meet
about your tragic story,
how you experienced the sturm
und drang of Purgatory.

Remember, after winning someone's
honest sympathy
without equivocation, only
then will you be free.'

I questioned his sincerity,
but in the end believed
his act of charity was true,
compelling me to trust that you
should give as you received.

And so I drank his offering,
when gradually his beard
began to morph, transforming 'til
a live cartoon appeared.

I saw a band of tiny devils
hoofing down a street,
and I was leading them along
to 'Auld Lang Syne' but it was wrong,
they ruined the rhythm of the song—
Bang! Clang! Tweet!

The flutists tweeting marching with
percussionists who clanged
created a cacophony
as clashing drummers banged.

My ears were aching from the noise.
Assaulted by a flash,
my eyes were blinded followed by
a whistling sound somewhere up high
that dive-bombed with a *splash!*

Eventually my sight returned.
The Stranger and the crew
and I were all positioned to
appreciate the view.

PART 12 – Unhappy New Year

Chicago's midnight waterfront
erupted just ahead
with roman candles, flares and rockets
yellow, green and red.

We had arrived with fanfare at
our final destination
in time to witness at its best
a New Year's celebration.

The sights and sounds distracted me
throughout the noisy night,
until a morning fog rolled in
that muffled the subsiding din
and scattered all the light.

The Stranger turning to Priscilla
told her to proceed.
At first she hesitated then
reluctantly agreed.

In all our crazy times together,
civilized and wild,
I never saw her look so sad.
She tried but never smiled.

She stopped, stood, for one solemn
second stared before
she prophesied, 'You know, I'll never
see you anymore.'

With unassuming ceremony
she began untying
the rope as tears welled in her eyes;
despite her effort to disguise
I saw that she was crying.

She finished loosening the rope,
then made a courtly bow
inviting me to step away.
My body stayed somehow

against the crucifying mast,
my body didn't drop.
The Stranger clapped—I separated
with a piercing *pop*

and crumpled to the deck immobile
at Priscilla's feet.
Exhausted, I felt helpless in my
moment of defeat.

In earnest she began to string
the rope around my body,
enunciating, 'Like a bee
is busy busy busy me
entombing scientifically.'
She finished then asserted, 'See,
this rope outlines a potty.'

She was of course referring to
the tombstone at the head,
the toilet bowl where I had found
my thirsty crew all dead.

Priscilla stepped inside and placed
her body next to mine.
She cuddled closer pining, 'I
was once your valentine.'

The Stranger scolded her, 'Enough!
We have no time for that.'
She looked at him, she looked at me,
then with a feline snarl she
attacked me like a cat.

The Stranger quickly pulled her off
and wrestled her aside.
'It isn't fair!' Priscilla griped,
'He lived and us? We died!'

'A valid point,' the Stranger said,
'the way you had been treated.
I too expected better things
and feel just as cheated.'

Their grievances reflected mine,
the philosophic kind,
an indistinct elusive itch
that irritates the mind:

The memes inherited from friends
and family that nurture
our worldview can inhibit us
from mastering our future

when we dispute with faulty facts
or argue from the heart,
or disregard hard evidence
and quit before we start.

Societies enlist us with
their hallowed history
from godless communism to
the theocentric view that's true
of Christianity.

Historic themes revealed in dreams
as symbols, sights and sounds,
reflect beliefs that we accept
where nothing's out of bounds—

Beliefs in Hell, the Greater Good,
in fairies, devils, gods,
purporting they are right and true.
I ask, what are the odds?

Not much, I think. We should abide
by Nature, take our chances
and challenge settled systems as
society advances.

Reject the memes, the scams and schemes
that teach us how to feel.
Instead, if truth is what we love
then trust in us, believe that we
will consummate our destiny—
the übermensch! a product of
our dominant allele,

the rising son who represents
the future of *our* kind.
The Stranger and his minions will
in contrast fall behind

because their leader's posturing
and exercise of reason
exposed his mighty masquerade—
a man without a season.

Priscilla, on the other hand,
I'm not ashamed to say
displayed believability.
I loved her in a way.

The Stranger he examined me
to see what she had done.
My scratches showed that I had bled,
proof positive I wasn't dead.
Competing for my life, instead
of Nurture, Nature won.

Distracted by the bird perched on
the top yard of my cross,
the Stranger, flush with anger at
the agent of his loss,

pooh-poohed the bird by gesturing,
then pointed to the shore
where smoke from fireworks condensed.
I'd seen it once before!

A gateway where a scarlet mist
throbbed like a beating heart;
it floated closer 'til we were
a dozen waves apart.

Then everyone collected on
the port side as it neared,
and jumped across the distance.
In a blink they disappeared!

Priscilla, Carmen, Stanislaw
plus Clark and Emily
joined by the Stranger one and all,
of course except for me.

Then just as quick the gate was gone
to Heaven? Dreamland? Where?
The answer was a dissonant
I care! I care! I care!

My guardian perched overhead,
committed, watched my back,
then suddenly that bird did drop
and everything turned black.

PART 13 – American Standard

It seemed forever, lying on
the deck day after day.
The very most that I discerned
was shadowy and gray.

One day it rained, I felt the drops
like bullets on my skin.
One day the sun came out, it felt
like spring would soon begin.

One day I heard a frog, he sang
an April melody.
One day I heard the whistling wind,
One day a rustling tree.

One day a child called, 'Look at
that funny man out there!'
One day the smell of beer and spicy
spareribs filled the air.

One day I heard a rumbling train.
One day I heard a bell.
One day the air was soured by
a pungent oil well.

I jerked my head up off the deck
and opened up my eyes.
Befuddled like a patient after
being etherized,

the stacks and towers that I saw
with their familiar glow
at last explained themselves to me.
Shalott was on the eerie sea
approaching Buffalo!

My heart cried out to tell the world,
I'm back! Hello! Shalom!
I've been away too long and now
at last I'm coming home!

Thanks to the wind, a westerly
that all year long prevailed,
Shalott was ushered near the shore
where we so many times before
had set a course and sailed.

Now, could it be from Pelee Point
west to the Windy City,
and all the plots and places in
between from great to gritty—

could it be all my struggles were
imagined, nothing more?
the consequence of having landed
on the cabin floor?

sustaining injuries that added
insult to my mind?
If so, then just off Pelee Point
the west wind had been kind,

propelling me due east, the lone
survivor of the cruise.
Unfortunately now the wind
was bringing me bad news,

no longer what I wished to hear,
instead a hellish howl,
a disappointing welcoming.
I wanted to cry Foul!

There is a sailor saying: To
survive a sudden gale
it takes a quantity of skill,
a dose of luck, and if you will,
a measure of white whale.

To keep from slipping off the deck
I reached and hugged the mast
as wind and waves lambasted me.
I feared I wouldn't last.

I didn't! My sweet yacht Shalott,
caught by a monster breaker,
crashed on a sunken seawall sending
me to meet my maker—

The primal sea whose chemistry
had mixed a potent brew
from which we all evolved producing
me as well as you.
===
The Mariner takes in a breath,
"Of course, I didn't drown.
Somehow I reached the stormy shore—
What is it? Why the frown?"

"It isn't fair," Sylvester claims,
"the way you suffered so."
The Mariner with gravitas
reflects, "Too well I know."

Referring to the den Sylvester
asks him, "Be my guest?
The night's been long for both of us.
Let's go where we can rest."

The Mariner emphatically
responds, "To that I'll drink!"
He offers him the bottle with
a calculated wink.

Disposed to gullibility,
Sylvester growing weary
drinks up! then he is puzzled by
a strange look in the Mariner's eye
that causes him to query:

"Did I mess up? Say something wrong?
Why look at me that way?
I hope you didn't change your mind.
Please promise me you'll stay."

"I will," the Mariner replies,
"because *I care* for you."
Sylvester, heartened, ventilates,
"And I care for you too!"

The Mariner erupts with joy,
"At last! You set me free!"
He pushes off the startled druggie,
plunges in the sea

and with Olympic stamina
he swims away from shore.
Sylvester screams, "Oh no, don't go!"
to his lost visitor.

Another shock awaits Sylvester
out there in the night.
He sees emerging from the water
something moonlit white:

An entity with broad dimensions
clearly off the chart,
approaching swiftly leading with
its bulbous forward part,

appearing not unlike the way
a whale would behave
that plunges, surfaces and creases
every swell and wave.

When it comes closer to the shore
it pauses, dips then rises,
revealing what can only be
described as an absurdity,
the mother of surprises.

The Mariner is standing on
its rim around the hole
of the impossible, a white
titanic toilet bowl!

The Mariner salutes Sylvester,
waves, then topples back
in to the bowels of his tomb;
the toilet lid slams with a *boom*
loud as a bomb attack.

The flabbergasted druggie flinches,
then the bowl is hit
by lightning causing it to sink
so fast he hasn't time to think!
He nearly has a fit.

Another lightning strike alerts
him to the danger there.
Hysterical, he runs away
from his life-changing scare,

back up the shore, back to his den
beyond the distant dune.
He charges through the driving rain
intent to be home soon.

And soon enough he's at the dune.
He clambers to the crest
then bounces down the leeward slope
hell-bent like one possessed.

One minute more and he'll be home
but lightning strikes the den!
A fire starts, a conflagration
stunning him and then...

the den explodes! It disappears
in one mind-blowing flash!
In evidence are odors of
a lab for meth and hash.

Completely overwhelmed, Sylvester
stands before the rubble
absent buddies—nothing! Just
the artifacts of trouble.

The storm subsides. The Sun decides
to start a brighter day.
Sylvester preps to leave, but first
before he makes his way,

he pulls a packet from his pocket.
Resolute, he tosses
the packet labeled *Magic Mushrooms*
covering his losses.

He leaves a wiser man, cleansed by
his purifying act,
determined next time to distinguish
fantasy from fact.

===

NOTES

PART 1 – High Moon

eerie inland sea – Lake Erie is the fourth largest lake by surface area of the five Great Lakes in North America.

druggie – An individual who habitually uses illicit drugs.

dominant allele – An alternative form of the same gene producing different effects. Its dominance is manifested by masking the expression of another allele at the same location on a chromosome.

turtleneck – A garment with a high, tubular collar, frequently rolled down that fits closely about the neck.

PART 2 – Bon Voyage Not

Lady of Shalott – Title of a Victorian ballad by Alfred, Lord Tennyson. The Lady of Shalott lives in a castle on an island in a river which flows to Camelot. She suffers from a curse, obliged to continually weave images on her loom without ever looking out at the world. Instead, she looks into a mirror which reflects the world outside. The reflected images are a poor substitute for seeing directly. The lady stops weaving and looks out a window toward Camelot, disregarding the curse. She leaves her tower, finds a boat upon which she writes her name, and floats down the river. She dies before arriving at the palace where Sir Lancelot, among others, witnesses her passing.

petty pace – The phrase refers to Macbeth's soliloquy in William Shakespeare's tragedy. Macbeth concludes life is devoid of meaning and full of struggles, comparable to a person performing a minor role on stage in an absurd play.

monohull – The most prevalent form of waterborne vessel having only one hull.

Spirit class – A designation of the Modern Mariner's yacht Shalott, an anthropomorphized entity with spiritual qualities. Real yachts of course must conform to recognized standards to be insurable at competitive rates against liability claims; therefore, they are duly classified.

Buffalo – A city located in northwestern New York on the eastern shore of Lake Erie.

Chicago – A city located in northeastern Illinois on the southwestern shore of Lake Michigan.

Ohio – A state in the Midwestern United States. Much of its northern border is defined by the southern limit of Lake Erie.

Cleveland – A city located in northeastern Ohio on the shore of Lake Erie.

La algarada – An outcry or uproar.

Cuyahoga – A river located in northeast Ohio, its terminus emptying into Lake Erie. In the past, fires have been reported burning on the river polluted by flammables including oil.

waterspout – An intense columnar vortex usually appearing as a funnel-shaped cloud that occurs over a body of water; similar to a tornado.

Michigan – A state in the Great Lakes region of the United States. Michigan has the longest freshwater coastline of any political subdivision in the world.

peninsula – Land that projects into a body of water and is connected with a larger landmass. The state of Michigan comprises two peninsulas, the Upper and Lower. They are separated by the Straits of Mackinac, a channel that joins Lake Michigan to Lake Huron.

hand – The Lower Peninsula of Michigan is often noted to be shaped like a mitten or left hand.

head – Refers to the toilet compartment of a ship.

PART 3 – Pelee Point Counterpoint

scow – A flat-bottomed boat with a blunt bow capable of sailing into shallow waters, an advantage over keeled vessels. A scow, however, loses seaworthiness in open water and inclement weather.

Pelee Point – The tip of a peninsula in Point Pelee National Park located in southwestern Ontario, a province of Canada. The peninsula consists of land that tapers to a sharp point as it extends into Lake Erie.

butterflies – Point Pelee is a world famous location for viewing monarch butterfly migrations. The location is the shortest crossing point over Lake Erie for butterflies during their journey to their winter home in the mountains of central Mexico.

Mayan snake – Refers to a Maya deity depicted as a feathered serpent closely related to Quetzalcoatl of the Aztecs.

halyard – A rope used to hoist a sail, flag, or spar on a mast from which sails are set.

PART 4 – Trick or Treat

Zen – A meditative state where practitioners may assume prescribed sitting positions and concentrate on breathing to regulate the mind.

Detroit – A city located in southeastern Michigan on the Detroit River.

Motor City – Nickname for the city of Detroit.

Old Mariners' Church – Located in the downtown district of Detroit. The church holds an annual Blessing of the Fleet Service for those embarking on sea voyages, and a Great Lakes Memorial Service for those who have lost their lives at sea.

The Crow – A comic book series created by James O'Barr. According to legend, the crow has the power to resurrect the dead, affording them with the opportunity to correct an injustice.

tunnel – A highway tunnel under the Detroit River that connects Detroit, Michigan in the United States, with Windsor, Ontario in Canada.

Devil's Night – A name associated with October 30, the night before Halloween when citizens engage in a night of criminal behavior, usually consisting of acts of petty vandalism. However, in the early 1970s, vandalism escalated to seriously destructive acts, especially arson. This primarily occurred in the inner city of Detroit. The destruction peaked with more than 800 fires set in 1984. Devil's Night is an integral part of the 1994 film *The Crow*.

Windsor Star – A regional daily newspaper of Windsor, a city in the Ontario province of Canada. The city is located south across the river from Detroit.

PART 5 – Hang Over

Death's Door – A navigational passage linking Green Bay with Lake Michigan. It lies between the northern tip of the peninsula of Door County, Wisconsin and a group of islands. The name in French, "Porte des Mortes," literally means "the door of the dead." Death's Door Spirits, a distillery located in Middleton, Wisconsin, offers as one of its products, a flavorful gin.

Lake Saint Claire – A freshwater lake that lies between the Canadian province of Ontario and the state of Michigan, northeast of the downtown districts of Detroit, Michigan and Windsor, Ontario.

S.O.B. – A vulgarity meaning son of a bitch.

Huron – Lake Huron is the second largest by surface area of the five Great Lakes in North America.

Straits of Mackinac – The narrow waterway separating the state of Michigan's Lower Peninsula from its Upper Peninsula. The straits connect Lake Michigan and Lake Huron.

Saint Marys River – Drains Lake Superior, starting at the southeastern corner of Whitefish Bay, then flowing southeast into Lake Huron. The entire length of the river is an international border, separating Michigan in the United States from Ontario in Canada.

Soo Locks – A set of locks which enables ships to travel between Lake Superior and the lower Great Lakes. The locks are located on the Saint Marys River, where the rapids are bypassed as the water falls approximately 7 meters.

Lake Superior – The largest of the Great Lakes of North America. It is generally considered the largest freshwater lake in the world by surface area.

PART 6 – Apostle Impossible

lead – A large fracture within an expanse of sea ice, defining a linear area of open water usable for navigation purposes.

polynya – An extensive area of open water surrounded by sea ice.

ice volcanoes – When an ice layer forms along a shore line, the incoming waves push through, causing a volcano shaped cone to develop on the top of the ice layer. Waves crashing under the cones cause water to erupt through the top, suggestive of erupting volcanoes.

sturgeon – A freshwater fish with a partly cartilaginous skeleton, its overall streamlined shape resembles an armored torpedo. The skin on the back and sides of the fish bear rows of bony plates called scutes rather than scales.

Apostle Islands – A group of 22 islands in Lake Superior, off the Bayfield Peninsula in northern Wisconsin. All the islands except for Madeline are part of the Apostle Islands National Lakeshore. They were named the Apostles because of the 12 largest islands.

PART 7 – Scheming Dreams

sandstone – Lake Superior Sandstone belongs to the Bayfield Group of Cambrian or Upper Proterozoic sandstones. The Chequamegon formation underlies all of the Apostle Islands.

OZ – Refers to "The Wonderful Wizard of Oz," a children's novel written by L. Frank Baum and illustrated by W. W. Denslow. OZ also refers to "Ozymandias," the title of a sonnet by Percy Bysshe Shelley.

Dorothy – The main character in the Wizard of Oz story. She is knocked unconscious during a storm. She experiences magical events during her unconsciousness, eventually recovering and facing reality once again.

Ozymandias – A "king of kings," he was the subject of a sonnet by Percy Bysshe Shelley. Ozymandias can be viewed as a metaphor for the pride and hubris of humanity.

Temple Gate – A rock formation shaped like an arch, located immediately offshore from Sand, one of the Apostle Islands.

PART 8 – Gate Fate

Sea of Tranquility – A lunar mare located within the Tranquillitatis basin on the Moon.

PART 9 – Guilt Trip

Mace – A type of aerosol potent enough (when sprayed in the face) to act as a credible deterrent and incapacitant.

vivid dream – A sensation during a dreaming episode so intense it is difficult to determine if the experience is real or not.

PART 10 – Fright Christmas

lighthouse – The oldest active light on Lake Superior features a central structure supported by a skeletal framework, designed to relieve stress caused by high winds. The lighthouse is home to the Great Lakes Shipwreck Museum which displays many shipwreck artifacts.

Whitefish Bay – Located on the eastern end of the southern shore of Lake Superior between Michigan and Ontario. The international boundary runs through the bay which is heavily used by shipping traffic northbound and southbound from the Soo Locks. Whitefish Bay became the site of numerous shipwrecks, many of which are protected for future generations of sports divers by the Whitefish Point Underwater Preserve.

Fitz – Nickname for the *SS Edmund Fitzgerald,* an American Great Lakes freighter that sank in a Lake Superior storm. The sinking of the freighter is one of the most famous disasters in the history of Great Lakes shipping. Gordon Lightfoot, a Canadian singer-songwriter, made it the subject of his 1976 hit ballad "The Wreck of the Edmund Fitzgerald."

Canadian lock – A single small lock on the Canadian side of the Soo, used for recreational and tour boats.

American locks – A set of locks on the U.S. side of the Soo, owned and maintained by the United States Army Corp of Engineers, which provides free passage for major shipping traffic.

Saint Nicholas – An historic 4th-century saint and Greek Bishop. He had a reputation for secret gift giving, such as putting coins in the shoes of those who would leave them out for him. He thus became the model for Santa Claus.

DeTour Village – A village located at the extreme eastern tip of the Upper Peninsula of Michigan, at the turning point for the shipping channel that connects the Saint Marys River with Lake Huron and the Straits of Mackinac.

bridge – The Mackinac Bridge is a suspension bridge spanning the Straits of Mackinac. It connects the Upper and Lower peninsulas of Michigan.

across – Sometimes pronounced "acrosst" with a "t."

final inland sea – Lake Michigan is the only Great Lake located entirely within the United States boundary. It is the third largest by surface area.

animus – A hostile attitude. In Jungian psychology, the masculine principle present in the female unconscious.

Beaver Island – The largest island in Lake Michigan and part of the Beaver Island archipelago, once home to a unique American monarchy.

James Jesse Strang – An American religious leader, politician and self-proclaimed monarch who founded the Church of Jesus Christ of Latter Day Saints (Strangite), a faction of the Latter Day Saint movement. He was a major contender for leadership of the Church during the 1844 succession crisis following the murder of its founder. Strang was rejected, prompting him to start his own sect. He reigned for six years as the crowned "king" of an ecclesiastical monarchy that he established on Beaver Island in Lake Michigan. Building an organization that eventually rivaled Brigham Young's in Utah, Strang gained nearly 12,000 adherents prior to his murder in 1856, which brought down his kingdom and all but extinguished his sect.

Draco – The first legislator of Athens in Ancient Greece. He replaced the prevailing system of oral law and blood feud by a written code enforceable only by a court. Known for its harshness, draconian has come to refer to unforgiving rules or laws.

Ruby Ridge – The site of a deadly confrontation and siege in Idaho, which occurred in 1992 against Randy Weaver, his family and Weaver's friend Kevin Harris, by agents of the United States Marshals Service (USMS) and Federal Bureau of Investigation (FBI). It resulted in the death of Weaver's son Sammy, his wife Vicki and Deputy U.S. Marshal William Francis Degan.

In response to public criticism about Ruby Ridge, the U.S. Senate Subcommittee on Terrorism, Technology and Government Information issued a report calling for reforms in federal law enforcement to prevent a repeat of Ruby Ridge and to restore public confidence in federal law enforcement.

Waco – Also known as the *Waco Massacre*. It was a siege of a compound belonging to the religious group Branch Davidians. The siege was conducted by American federal and Texas state law enforcement and military. It occurred between February 28 and April 19, 1993. The Christian sect, led by David Koresh, lived at Mount Carmel Center ranch near Waco, Texas. The group was suspected of weapons violations. A search and arrest warrant was obtained.

The incident began when the Bureau of Alcohol, Tobacco and Firearms (ATF) attempted to raid the ranch. An intense gun battle erupted, resulting in the deaths of four agents and six Branch Davidians. The ATF's failure to raid the compound was followed by a siege initiated by the Federal Bureau of Investigation (FBI). The standoff lasted 51 days. Eventually, the FBI launched an assault and initiated a tear gas attack in an attempt to force out the Branch Davidians. During the attack, a fire engulfed Mount Carmel Center and 76 men, women and children, including David Koresh, died.

PART 11 – Caring is Believing

I care! – The sound of a crow calling, allowing for poetic license; in reality better expressed as *caw!*

power plant – The Palisades Power Plant is a nuclear facility located on the western lake shore of the state of Michigan.

silver carp – A variety of freshwater Asian fish. They were imported to North America to control algae growth in commercial and municipal facilities. The highly invasive silver carp is also called the flying carp for its tendency to leap from the water when startled.

sturm und drang – A phrase that suggests suffering. It also refers to a romantic movement in German literature, characterized chiefly by exaltation of the individual, rejection of established forms and nationalism.

Purgatory – A place of suffering or remorse.

Auld Lang Syne – A Scots poem by Robert Burns set to the tune of a traditional folk song. It is traditionally used to celebrate the start of the New Year at the stroke of midnight.

PART 12 – Unhappy New Year

valentine – One or more early Christian saints named Valentinus. Valentine's Day is observed once each year. The day was first associated with romantic love. It evolved into an occasion in which lovers expressed their love for each other with sentimental offerings.

memes – An idea, behavior, or style that spreads from person to person within a culture. A meme acts as a unit for carrying cultural ideas, symbols, or practices that can be transmitted from one mind to another through writing, speech, gestures, rituals, or other imitable phenomena.

Greater Good – Refers to the principle of the end justifying the means. Basically, one should not rationalize one's behavior by exploiting other people to satisfy one's own ends.

übermensch – A superior person, superhuman as it were. The philosopher Friedrich Nietzsche posited the übermensch as a goal to which humanity should aspire in his 1883 book *Thus Spake Zarathustra*.

man without a season – Refers to "A Man For All Seasons," the title of a play by Robert Bolt. The play portrays the accomplished Englishman Sir Thomas More as a man true to himself despite external pressure or influence.

gateway – A magical or technological portal that connects two distant locations separated by spacetime. Gateways are similar to the cosmological concept of a wormhole, also known as an Einstein-Rosen Bridge, which is a hypothetical topological feature that would be a "shortcut" through spacetime.

PART 13 – American Standard

Windy City – Nickname for the city of Chicago.

lab for meth – A clandestine lab where the methamphetamine drug is manufactured. Solvents used in the process may evaporate. Confined to a poorly ventilated space, the flammable air can explode when ignited by a spark such as lightning.

Magic Mushrooms – Also known as psychedelic mushrooms. After ingestion, the mind-altering effects are considerable. Some users report experiencing the single most spiritually significant moment of their lives.

★ Stephen Kryska ★

MAP

INLAND SEAS
(Great Lakes)

1 - Buffalo	6 - Lake St. Claire	10 - Mackinac Bridge
2 - Cleveland	7 - Apostle Islands	11 - Beaver Island
3 - Pelee Point	8 - Whitefish Bay	12 - Power Plant
4 - Detroit	9 - Soo Locks	13 - Chicago
5 - Windsor		

GENESIS

POEM – Stephen Kryska suffered a minor setback in the year 1961. As an enlistee in the United States Air Force, he was stationed at Lackland Air Force Base in San Antonio, Texas. He attended a class off base at a local university. The subject of the class was English Literature, which included an examination of Samuel Taylor Coleridge's "The Rime of the Ancient Mariner." One of Stephen's classmates was an attractive young woman who interested him. She, however, never returned the compliment. Rejecting his advances toward her, he felt compelled to vent his frustration by composing a doggerel that he never delivered. Here it is unadorned:

> There was an Argonaut in quest
> For the golden fleece of yore.
> He sailed in his submarine
> With periscope aimed at a dream,
> Never near a shore.
>
> Brave Jim, the Argonaut, he had
> A little wife once named S. D.
> And everywhere that Jimmy went,
> Everywhere his time was spent
> S. D. would never be.
>
> Poor Stella, left in every port
> Whence her famous man departed,
> She retreated to her home,
> To her trailer house alone,
> For Jim a sweater she started.

It was to be a magic cloth
With golden sleeves and golden vest,
Golden neck with golden seam
To lure Jim from his golden dream,
She knitted without rest.

One fine day brave Jim returned,
But absent was his jolly air.
Stella gave that lonesome look
And walked into a resting nook,
Jim gave an empty stare.

Oh, her man as she could tell,
After his return from sail,
Did not have his glowing face,
All the glow was spent in chase,
The chase left his heart pale.

Jim's thoughts were on the golden fleece,
His spirit in the submarine.
He said, "Hello, now I must go
Where the waters raging flow,
Where the blue meets green."

Like painted words on painted lips
He said, "goodbye" and shut the door.
Stella rushed to say goodbye,
But her Jim was gone from eye.
Will he return no more?

Water, water, everywhere,
Oh, how the shores do shrink!
Water, water, everywhere,
Jim's sailing in the drink.

Ten years passed and Stella had
Finished knitting Jimmy's sweater,
Hoping to keep her man home
For she was dreadfully alone.
Ah, life will be much better!

Then captain Jim returned again
To their little trailer home.
He stayed awhile to say hello.
The sweater, before she could show,
He went off more to roam.

For the fleece was in his eye
Which made Jimmy sail the more.
It must be sought and be his gain
If to the raging bounty main
Or the earth's corners four.

Water, water, everywhere,
Oh, how the shores do shrink!
And her Jimmy's in his sub
Sailing in the drink.

Now it was their twentieth year
Since Stella and brave Jimmy wed.
Stella had grown old and gray,
Grayer since this was the day
When they first went to bed.

Hark! "Who knocks upon the door?"
Little lonesome Stella said.
"It is I, your husband, Dear."
Stella jumped and held her tear
Then to the door she sped.

She flung it open with surprise.
There stood Jim, a broken man
For he was old and he was worn,
Sad, and tired, and forlorn.
Salt tears from his cheeks ran.

Stella took the golden sweater
That for years she had been knitting,
Gave it to her husband thin
Who returned her with a grin
And to the rocking chair went sitting.

Jim's eyes were bright for now he found
The golden fleece that he searched for.
He pulled into the golden cotton,
Hugged his wife he loved the more,
But whose name he had forgotten.
Nevermore.

Stephen composed the doggerel with surprising ease, encouraging him to attempt a serious and ambitious version. His creative effort resulted in a draft comprised of over 432 stanzas, where the plot and format approximated Coleridge's "Ancient Mariner."

While stationed at an Air Force installation in Ankara, Turkey, Stephen revised his draft, introducing two major themes: (1) The imperative of striving for perfection at most, or personal improvement at least, suggestive of the philosopher Friedrich Nietzsche and (2) The supremacy of reason over faith and tradition, exemplified by the Enlightenment, the cultural movement that promoted scientific thought.

Coleridge's Ancient Mariner tells his story to a "Wedding-Guest," a listener who reacts like a "three years' child." Keying off this character description by Coleridge, Stephen imagined his Modern Mariner's listener would also react like a three years' child. Stephen was reminded of a famous quote from the classic fairy tale *Peter Pan*. The quote was incorporated into the Prologue to his draft:

> When the Lord God created the heaven and the earth, he said, "It is good."
>
> Then the Lord God fashioned, in his own image, clay from the earth and created Adam. Again he said, "It is good."
>
> Then the Lord God delivered a rib from Adam's side, and Eve was born. He said, "It is good."
>
> When Adam awoke, after the delivery, and realized that he was, in effect, the mother of the Mother of Mankind, Adam said, "It is weird."
>
> Later, after Eve gave birth to their first baby, she realized that she was, in effect, the daughter of a mother who was also her father and who happened to be her husband. So Eve said to Adam, "It is very weird."
>
> Cain laughed.

"When the first baby laughed for the first time, the laugh broke into a thousand pieces and they all went skipping about, and that was the beginning of fairies." *from Peter Pan* by J. M. Barrie

With *Peter Pan* in mind, Stephen decided the Modern Mariner should tell his story to a fairy. This proved unworkable. Following his retirement, Stephen revisited his draft and solved the problem. Thus, Sylvester was conceived.

Stephen imagined Sylvester as a flighty fellow, influenced by drugs and susceptible to irrational thought. In the end, Sylvester transforms into (1) an "übermensch lite" so to speak, besides (2) someone who recognizes the value of rationality.

By rejecting the mind-altering mushrooms, Sylvester's personal decision is particularly relevant for the times, given the permissive state of American culture circa 2013. After several months of discussion and rewrites, the result was the poetic fantasy *Rime of the Modern Mariner: An American Odyssey*.

POET – Stephen Kryska was born in Hamtramck, Michigan, in the year 1939, the oldest of four children. Follow his personal odyssey:

Stephen's father, Steve C. Kryska, was a bawdy jokester and high school dropout. He earned a living as a millwright, supplementing his income by operating a lottery (aka the numbers or policy racket). Never a hunter, he nonetheless owned a rifle, explaining he would use it to shoot rats that infested the alley behind his house on a residential street in Detroit. Rumor has it Steve was once stopped by legal authorities who searched his car for evidence related to his lottery business. The car seats were removed in the process. Steve refused to leave the scene with his car, which was obstructing traffic, until after the investigators reinstalled the seats. His parents were Stanislaw Kryska and Agniezka Gładysiak who emigrated from the Polish village of Łanięta in the year 1910. Stanislaw initially worked in a Pennsylvania coal mine, then as a machinist in a Michigan auto factory.

Stephen's mother, Florence A. Skiera, was a quiet daughter of a Michigan farmer. She lived in the town of Cheboygan while she attended high school, working as a housekeeper. Widowed when her oldest son Stephen was ten years old, she supplemented her Social Security income by continuing the operation of her husband's lottery business for a year. She retired as an industrial seamstress, managing to leave a modest inheritance to her four children. Her parents were John C. Skiera (a sometime member of a school board) and Sophie Grubinski. John's mother was Josephine Budzinski of Wisconsin. John's father was Frank Skiera who emigrated with his parents from the Polish village of Łobzenica circa 1872. Sophie's parents were Pawel Grubienski and Barbara Najman, who emigrated from the Polish village of Zelgno in the late 1800s.

Stephen grew up in a working class neighborhood in Detroit, dominated by ethnic Poles, Italians and Greeks. Fortunately, his worldview was expanded by his living on the farm of his maternal grandparents during summer vacations from school. He performed familiar tasks including milking cows, shocking wheat and plowing fields driving a tractor. Some relatives on the farm were musically inclined. He emulated them by learning to play the fiddle, which led him to write songs in typical 1950s fashion such as the following. Listen to a teenage girl's entreaty to her friend:

Ask the guy when he's passing by,
does he love me, does he care.
Does he ever think about me,
does he have some time to share.

Don't forget, remind him how we met,
of the things he promised me.
He told me he'd call on the phone.
I've been waiting patiently.

It was at the dance a week ago
when he said we'd meet again.
So I gave my number, now I'm waiting
patiently since then.

Ask the guy, Ask the guy,
Ask the guy if he loves me.

Ask the guy when he's passing by,
does he love me, he's my goal.
Ask him please is his silence a tease,
does he want my heart and soul.

If you find I'm never on his mind,
won't you tell me, set me free.
Cause I must know if he wants to go,
I can't wait endlessly.

Stephen was also an amateur herpetologist. His avocation
was sparked at an early age by his encounter with a snake
while he, his father, and his father's father were mushroom
picking in a suburban woodland. Here is one of Stephen's
field notes:

<u>Acris crepitana Blanchard</u>:(5/?/57) Brighton Scout Camp: 1:00 pm. Venturing upon a group of male <u>Acris</u> in chorus at a pond's edge, the following was observed:

An obvious male began to call. After a few minutes it abruptly lifted one of its hind legs into the air and then it would slowly fan its leg in sweeping motions right angle to the long axis of its body. It would then resume its normal squat. After walking a few inches the frog then hopped about 2' from the place where it was first discovered. Once again it committed the same act. The antics took place among the sparse tufts of grass covering the dark clay soil of the pond's edge. Another male <u>Acris</u> was observed calling but did not carry on as the first frog mentioned—the latter was sitting on a log about 4' from shore.

Stephen was a popular student in a parochial high school where he served as captain of the football team. He earned an athletic scholarship at the University of Detroit, but never won a varsity letter. He did, however, dress for a game against the United States Air Force Academy football team.

Stephen enlisted in the Air Force in the year 1960. He served as an assistant to a medical illustrator at the Lackland Air Force Base training hospital in San Antonio, Texas. He completed his four-year military obligation as a graphic artist at a logistics headquarters in Ankara, Turkey. There he was awarded the title "Airman of the Quarter."

He was honorably discharged and returned to Michigan. For several years he worked in the advertising field copywriting for a retailer and trafficking at an advertising agency. Later, he managed the production of a local newspaper in California, followed by a position as purchasing agent at a manufacturer. He returned to Michigan and worked as an assistant supervisor of a computer typesetting department at a printing company.

Computers piqued his interest, so he enrolled at a local college, where he earned an associate degree in Data Processing. There, he taught computer programming language classes part time. Eager to learn, he earned another associate degree in General Studies, and later a bachelor's degree in Business Administration. After several years employed at various establishments, where he performed tasks related to computer software and systems, he retired as an information technologist.

His wife Jane F. Meyer, a biology major in college and medical record analyst, hails from Joplin, Missouri, where they were married. Their union produced a daughter Emily, and a son Clark. Now Stephen enjoys his golden years composing country and gospel songs, besides researching his Polish family history.

The epitaph inscribed on the tombstone Stephen will share with his wife of many years is "Aim High," which coincidently is a major theme of the *Rime*.

CPSIA information can be obtained
at www.ICGtesting.com
Printed in the USA
LVOW10s0111231217
560596LV00017B/1471/P